Keeping Time

PRAISE FOR *STORYSHARES*

"One of the brightest innovators and game-changers in the education industry."
– Forbes

"Your success in applying research-validated practices to promote literacy serves as a valuable model for other organizations seeking to create evidence-based literacy programs."

- Library of Congress

"We need powerful social and educational innovation, and Storyshares is breaking new ground. The organization addresses critical problems facing our students and teachers. I am excited about the strategies it brings to the collective work of making sure every student has an equal chance in life."
– Teach For America

"Around the world, this is one of the up-and-coming trailblazers changing the landscape of literacy and education."
- International Literacy Association

"It's the perfect idea. There's really nothing like this. I mean wow, this will be a wonderful experience for young people."   - Andrea Davis Pinkney, Executive Director, Scholastic

"Reading for meaning opens opportunities for a lifetime of learning. Providing emerging readers with engaging texts that are designed to offer both challenges and support for each individual will improve their lives for years to come. Storyshares is a wonderful start."
- David Rose, Co-founder of CAST & UDL

Keeping Time

Sienna Santer

STORYSHARES

Story Share, Inc.
New York. Boston. Philadelphia

Storyshares
Story Share, Inc.
24 N. Bryn Mawr Avenue #340
Bryn Mawr, PA 19010-3304
www.storyshares.org

Inspiring reading with a new kind of book.

Interest Level: High School
Grade Level Equivalent: 5.7

9781642611625

Book design by Storyshares

Printed in the United States of America

Storyshares Presents

1

The group was an odd one.

A teenage boy leaned against the marble columns, his pants torn and smudged and his threadbare waistcoat barely covering his chest. No one knew who he was or cared to ask his name.

Ms. Anne Davis, a wealthy widow, immediately settled into an armchair and peeked at her appearance for the third time that morning. Her hand was shaking slightly as she held up the gold-plated pocket mirror.

A young immigrant couple stood silently away from the group. They were dressed in their finest clothing: she in her black skirt, cream blouse, and Sunday hat, and he in his tweed suit, which had been his grandfathers. *Were they Italian? Hungarian?* No one knew.

Another couple sashayed through the great oak bank doors: a movie producer with the Sunday edition, November 10th newspaper tucked under his arm and a pipe lazily drooping from the corner of his mouth, and his girlfriend Lucille, an actress with a glamorous dress and red clutch that matched her ruby lips, and cold, hawk-like green eyes that did not match her sweet demeanor. They settled into the love seat.

Each minded his or her own business, and each had no real interest in the others.

The teenage boy watched them all carefully.

2

"Ladies and gentlemen," the employee announced with a flourish, "please follow me into the elevator, and I will lead you to the vault." He pronounced elevator ele-vah-tor, at which the boy couldn't help but smirk. Pompous phony, he thought.

A single gleaming door stood at the end of the hall. Delicately balanced atop was a golden floor indicator, its solid brass arrow pointed at a shiny letter L.

A doorman turned the key to open the doors and everyone shuffled into the cramped enclosure. The boy graciously stepped aside to let them pass first.

The doorman shut the metal cage with a clang that echoed in the shaft below them. The elevator descended into the depths, clanking downwards until the last glimpse of light from above was snuffed. A shroud of darkness surrounded them, and the air felt as if it was mixed with ice. The immigrant woman screamed. She was claustrophobic and the tight elevator reminded her of the horrors of her childhood in the mines, when she would sink into the earth, praying that the last speck of sunlight was not her final glimpse of the world above. Her husband comforted her in another language. The employee huffed - he hated immigrants. Always so hard to communicate.

"Level V: Vault," the doorman said monotonously, and the cage came to a halt. As the door creaked open, the group emerged into the drafty corridor, the ladies' heels clicking ominously on the concrete floor.

In a nook in the wall was a kerosene lantern, which the employee lit using a match from his pocket. Shadows danced on the walls, inviting the group down the passageway.

Ms. Davis fingered the buttons of her mink coat. She crinkled her nose at the foul smell of the underground.

"For a San Francisco bank, you'd think they would keep it cleaner," she muttered, accentuating the last word and eyeing the bank employee with contempt. The immigrant woman next to her frowned in disapproval and silently switched to her husband's other arm. He fingered his pocket watch and wondered if he dared to check the time.

3

Just then, a bank employee strolled into the foyer, sporting a navy suit and perfectly groomed mustache. He had taken extra care to apply pomade this morning and styled it in the latest fashion. Ms. Davis thought he looked like her son, Harry, although Harry was much more handsome and the result of good breeding.

Glistening in the gloom, the vault door was a dull, heavy silver, rounded into a complete circle. A sleek handle, which looked like a boat wheel, protruded from the cool metal. Setting his hands on opposite sides of the lock, the bank employee turned it this way and that. It was an intricate maze only he knew the path to. One by one the metal bars surrounding the vault shot out like balls in a pinball machine, and the big door swung open.

The immigrant man was enraptured. His father had been a clock maker, and he had tinkered with locks and screws since he was a little boy. The vault door was the most beautiful and intricate mechanical wonder he had ever seen.

"This way, ladies and gentlemen." The employee ushered them through the entrance. To the left, a glass door led to a private viewing area with several sets of tables and chairs, a chandelier providing the only light. To the right was the spacious vault: a dark cavern surrounded by concrete, black lockboxes towering on shelves up to the ceiling like books stacked in a library. The air was icy and coated with moisture. The coolness of the gunmetal walls and floor seemed to seep through their shoes and prick their skin.

"Your valuables are under the utmost protection," the employee announced, waving his arm around in demonstration as he led them among the towering stacks. "Four hundred and fifty tons of concrete surround these walls on all three sides, and the surface is five hundred feet above us. The only entrance," he pointed back the way they had come, "is that vault door, designed by German engineer Johann Broigel. It is the finest in the world. Nothing can trigger the lock except an intricate routine of turns, which is known only to three people: the president of the bank, Johann Broigel, and myself. I can assure you that your precious valuables are safer than the King's jewels in the Tower of London." He chuckled, but no one joined him. The immigrant woman clapped her hands weakly as she stared wide-eyed at the spires of lockboxes surrounding them.

"Can we just view our boxes?" the producer huffed. He had a train to catch to Hollywood the next morning, and he needed his contract. Lucille was growing impatient. She had agreed to accompany him to the vault only if he agreed to take her to her favorite restaurant that night.

"Ah yes, certainly," the employee said, and he did not talk after that. He drew out a piece of paper from inside his coat, walked along the stacks, and pulled boxes sporadically from the shelves.

"Now, if you'll please follow me to the viewing area," he said, gesturing over his shoulder.

The employee distributed the boxes to their corresponding owners, noting whether each person was depositing, withdrawing, or viewing, and then opened each box with a set of keys.

4

Ms. Davis was the first to receive her box. It contained her priceless jewelry and dozens of bundles of paper notes she had received from her late husbands will. She, however, only had eyes for a small, silver bracelet in the back left corner. It had been given to her by her mother, and she in turn intended to pass it on to her granddaughter.

The immigrant couple fidgeted nervously with the lid of their box. They had been saving up for almost a year to bring their families to America, depositing nearly all of their paycheck each month into the lockbox for safe keeping. They finally had enough; this money was their families way to freedom.

The boy stood off to the side. He had not received his lockbox. He was trying unsuccessfully to catch the bank employee's attention when the producer asked if he could borrow the employee's pen.

"Yes, of course." The employee ignored the boy and drew the pen from his pocket, setting it on the table.

Just as the producer was about to pick it up, the pen twitched. It rolled from the table onto the ground. A tremor radiated through the vault. The chandelier plummeted from the ceiling, shattering into a thousand fragments of cut glass. The earth rumbled like a giant awakening from slumber.

"Earthquake!" the employee yelled.

The teenage boy dove under the table, dragging the immigrant woman and Ms. Davis with him. The producer bolted towards the exit, shoving people aside and knocking over tables and chairs. As he was about to escape through the vault door, the ceiling collapsed, and an avalanche of boulders and concrete cascaded in front of him, crashing onto the floor of the vault.

Just as suddenly as it had come, the shaking stopped. When the dust settled and they emerged from their hiding places, they saw with dismay that the exit was completely filled with rubble. The teenage boy clawed at the rocks and thrust his shoulders into the boulders.

"Help me!" he called, and the other three men hurled themselves against the wall of rock. It wouldn't budge.

The immigrant man spoke for the first time. "There's no way out."

The immigrant woman collapsed onto her knees and began to pray, bowing down at the ground.

"Oh, dear God, woman, you can't tell where Mecca is." The producer scowled at her.

Cant he tell she's Polish? the boy thought, rubbing his sore shoulder.

"Everyone remain calm," said the employee, looking the very opposite of calm himself. "We're going to find a way out."

"How?" the immigrant man asked.

"Well, um, I'm sure there's a way."

"No, you said yourself that was the only exit, and it is blocked."

The employee did not respond.

5

"You!" Lucille shouted, pointing her finger accusingly at the teenage boy. "You did this!"

The boy was aghast. "How did I do this? It was an earthquake!"

Lucille ignored him. "He's the suspicious one! What does he even need a lockbox for, anyway? He's nothing but a poor boy. How are we supposed to know he hasn't set off an explosion to distract us and steal our money?" she cried.

The bank employee frowned. He knew that the boy was by far the wealthiest person in the room, having just inherited a fortune from his prospector father, yet he chose to dress as if he was still working in the Sierra Nevadas. *Why cant he show more respect for the bank?* the employee thought.

"The boy's nothing but a child. He could never make up a scheme like that," Ms. Davis remarked. "He's probably too ignorant; he looks like he hasnt had proper schooling."

"I would never do something like this," the boy said finally, suppressing his anger. "But it did happen. We just have to hope that someone will come to dig us out. We can't contact anyone, so we have to trust that the doorman will remember that we're down here and call the firemen to come rescue us. It's a slim chance, but it's the best hope we have."

Everyone ignored his reassurances, shuffling to their own corners of the cavern and distancing themselves from the others. Ms. Davis fell asleep, clutching a picture of her son to her breast. The immigrant couple huddled together. Lucille sulked in a corner while the producer read his newspaper as far away from her as possible. He had enough of his own problems; he couldn't be bothered with her womanly trifles.

After a while they all began to get restless.

"What day is it?" Ms. Davis fanned herself with her hand. The imprint of her purse handle was ingrained into the side of her face as a result of using it as a pillow.

"The tenth of November, madam." The producer tapped the upper corner of his newspaper.

"How are we supposed to tell how long weve been stuck down here?"

"I have a watch," the boy said.

"Well, what time is it?" Ms. Davis asked impatiently.

The boy opened his mouth, and then stopped. "It's been two hours since the earthquake," he announced finally. "Why don't we assess what we have and see if there's anything of use."

They begrudgingly turned out their pockets and purses. Their collection consisted of: a lantern, a tube of red lipstick, a newspaper, a pipe, a pen, a pocket mirror, a rosary, a bottle of perfume, three handkerchiefs, a coin purse filled with Polish money, a pair of spectacles, a comb, and one gold pocket watch.

No one said anything. The employee opened his mouth and then shut it.

"No water and no food," Lucille stated several seconds later.

"We're going to die," the employee announced, shaking his head. No one challenged him, having each come to the same conclusion. The immigrant man comforted his trembling wife, his face grim. The producer paced furiously among the shelves while Lucille stared at the wall in shock.

After some time, Ms. Davis clutched her stomach. "I need food," she moaned.

"You can't be that hungry, it's only been a few hours," the employee said. "You only think you're starving because you know that there is nothing to eat."

"I actually feel full," the immigrant woman piped up, but then fell silent as she was met with resentful stares.

"How long have we been stuck here?" Lucile demanded after a while, turning to the teenage boy.

"It's only been twelve hours, ma'am."

"I don't believe you."

"Lucille, give it a rest. The boy has the watch, not you," the producer said lazily, turning over another page of his newspaper and pretending to read an ad for Daisy Deluxe perfume. Lucille glared at him and stamped her foot.

"It can't be only twelve hours. It feels like days! How am I supposed to know if Im dying of thirst?"

"You're not, ma'am. Humans can survive three to four days without water, and it's only been half of one. We'll be rescued before we starve," the boy answered. Ms. Davis wondered if he was trying to reassure himself as much as Lucille. He looked the worst of them all. His cheeks were pulled tightly against his face and his eyes glistened.

6

What felt like days passed by. The group grew more and more hungry. Their lips cracked from lack of water. Their stomachs ate away at their insides, searching for food that would never come.

Some time later, the immigrant woman stealthily dipped her hand into her pocket and produced a mint candy, attempting to shield it with her other hand. As she carefully unwrapped it, the paper crinkled. Everyone looked up.

"She has food!" yelled the producer.

The immigrant man snatched the candy from his wife's hand and tried to stuff it into his suit pocket to protect her. She wrestled it from his grip, but Lucille scratched the woman's face and tore her hair trying to reach it. The immigrant woman screamed and tripped. Ms. Davis pried the candy from her fingers. She unwrapped the mint completely and was about to place it triumphantly in her mouth when the producer slapped her hand, and the candy fell on the floor.

"How dare you take that from an old woman!" she shrieked.

"Stop! Stop!" shouted the bank employee, trying to pull everyone apart and in doing so, crushing the candy under his foot.

"Get the pieces!" Lucille yelled, and they all scrambled and screamed yet again, climbing over each other like wild animals.

"Everybody, stop!" yelled the boy, furiously kicking the pieces aside with his shoe. "There's no use fighting. We're all stuck here together, and no one person deserves to live more than the other. So," he said, picking up the candy pieces, "we're going to split it. Equally."

"How do we know you won't take more for yourself?" the immigrant man huffed.

"You're just going to have to trust me," the boy said, dropping a piece in everyone's outstretched hand, and placing the tiniest splinter in his own mouth. No one thanked him; they all turned away. The boy clenched his fists and curled up against his lockbox, wishing for his father and mother. *I'll see them soon*, he thought.

"How long has it been?" croaked Ms. Davis later.

"One day, ma'am," the boy replied sleepily.

"How long?"

"26 hours. It's November 11th."

"How long?"

"30 hours."

"How long?"

"Only a day and a half."

"But it feels like more."

"It's only been a day and a half, I promise you."

Keep going. Keep going. Keep going, they told themselves.

Their lips bled. Their stomachs felt as if knives were being thrust into them. Ms. Davis was so starved she choked down her lipstick, and the rest of the group hungrily munched on the paper documents. Lucille passed around a bottle of perfume, and they took turns sipping at its contents. It tasted like burnt flowers and scorched their insides.

Keep going. Keep going. Keep going.

7

They all huddled together between two stacks, resting their heads against the lockboxes.

"My son Harry doesn't speak to me anymore," Ms. Davis whispered into the dark. "He left home when he was sixteen. Now he lives with his wife and their daughter in Chicago. My grandbaby just turned eight years old, and I've never even seen her." A tear trickled down her cheek. She was glad that no one could see.

"My family is back in Poland. I haven't seen them in years. I know how you feel," whispered the immigrant man.

Lucille was crying quietly next to the immigrant woman, who squeezed her hand and asked her what was the matter. "I just want him to love me," Lucille whimpered, burying her head into her dress. "But he can barely even look at me anymore." The producer sat with his back to her, reading the same line in his newspaper over and over, listening to every word.

"My father and mother are dead," said the boy. "I have no family now." But no one heard him.

"How long?" The immigrant woman asked after a while.

The boy checked his watch. "40 hours."

Keep going. Keep going. Keep going.

It felt like an eternity. The lantern sputtered and died, and they were shut in complete darkness, together but alone.

Keep going. Keep going. Keep going.

"How long?" the employee asked frantically.

"45 hours," the boy answered.

"How long?"

"Two days. Its November 12th."

"Two days. Two days. One more day and we'll all be dead," the immigrant man muttered.

Away from the group, Lucille was resting against a shelf. "My dear, I have something to tell you," she gasped, clutching her stomach weakly. The producer grunted in acknowledgment but refused to look at her. "I'm pregnant."

Silence. "I was going to be a father?" the producer whispered, staring straight ahead, his expression unmoved.

"Yes," breathed Lucille, eyeing him fearfully.

The producers eyes filled with tears and he held his face in his hands for several moments before reaching over to Lucille and giving her a firm kiss. "I'm so sorry," he said, and hugged her tightly. Lucille sobbed into his chest.

Keep going. Keep going. Keep going.

They wondered if it would hurt to die, and if the pain could be any worse than what they were already feeling.

Their breathing became ragged and broken. Their bodies were numb. Their heartbeats slowed.

And then....

8

"Voices," murmured the employee.

"Your mind is playing tricks on you," Ms. Davis croaked.

"No, he's right!" shouted the producer. They all struggled to sit up, not yet willing to believe or to even hope.

A crack appeared in the boulder, and then another. The group clutched each other's hands as the wreckage came tumbling apart. A team of firemen stepped through the rubble.

"We found them!" one yelled. More men followed, carrying stretchers, and waving flashlights over the cavern, their beams coming to rest on all seven prisoners.

Ms. Davis was the first to be helped. She hugged the fireman who was about to lift her onto a stretcher.

"I'm going to see my Harry," she whispered, tears dripping down her cheeks. "I'm going home to my Harry."

The producer was so happy he kissed Lucille. They hobbled out together arm in arm, escorted by the firemen, but they never separated. Lucille's hair was a mess, she wasn't wearing any face powder, and her once pristine dress was covered in dirt stains. She couldn't care less.

The immigrant couple broke into the semblance of a Polish folkdance. The woman even kissed the feet of each of the firemen, despite their protests, muttering, "bless you, bless you." The man shook each of their hands affectionately. The employee was so parched he could barely speak, but he smiled and kept shaking his head in utter disbelief.

Everyone was too preoccupied to think of the boy. He was lying next to his empty lockbox, his head resting upon his arm. His eyes were shut and his lips formed a serene smile. He looked almost angelic.

He was dead.

And in his hand he clutched the watch. It was November 15, 10:33 am.

About The Author

Sienna Santer is a seventeen year old junior from San Luis Obispo, California. She takes classes from her local community college, AP courses online, and is also currently enrolled in Stanford University Online High School. Sienna's academic interests include English and creative writing, art and design, marine science, and business. At age fourteen, she wrote a 50,000 word novel on a month-long writing retreat with other teens, and at age fifteen, a short screenplay during a summer at Stanford University.

She is currently founding the Khan Global Fellows Program with Sal Khan and Khan Lab School, inviting teens to pursue a life of self agency and come together to solve global problems and foster a greater movement towards self-directed learning. Sienna volunteers feeding hungry families in her county through the collection of produce. Sienna incorporates history and language intensives into her curriculum, studying in England, France, and Spain within the last year. She has interned with Doctor Denise Herzing of the Wild Dolphin Project, studying dolphin communication, and is an animal-rights advocate and vegetarian. Sienna recently returned from a semester at Maine Coast Semester at Chewonki, where she studied environmentalism and sustainability with 40 other high school juniors in Maine. She hopes to study English or Creative Writing at university.

About The Publisher

Story Shares is a nonprofit focused on supporting the millions of teens and adults who struggle with reading by creating a new shelf in the library specifically for them. The ever-growing collection features content that is compelling and culturally relevant for teens and adults, yet still readable at a range of lower reading levels.

Story Shares generates content by engaging deeply with writers, bringing together a community to create this new kind of book. With more intriguing and approachable stories to choose from, the teens and adults who have fallen behind are improving their skills and beginning to discover the joy of reading. For more information, visit storyshares.org.

Easy to Read. Hard to Put Down.

Sienna Santer

www.ingramcontent.com/pod-product-compliance
Lightning Source LLC
Chambersburg PA
CBHW071229170626
46809CB00005BA/1988